To Lucy, our wise fetcher, friend, and comedian. We love you.

–L.C. and M.C.

To my son, Jorel, who fills my life with laughter and love.

–H.N.

Sebastian had two problems in soccer. First, he liked to talk a lot–to his teammates, his coach, and anyone standing around the big green field where he played, including the squirrels that raced up and down the limbs of the maple trees.

Bash and Lucy
Fetch Confidence

Enjoy!
Lisa + Michael Cohn

By Lisa & Michael Cohn
Illustrated by Heather Nichols

ISBN: : 0615809758
ISBN 13: 9780615809755
Library of Congress Control Number: 2013908284
Canines And Kids Publishing
Portland, OR

He talked from the second he climbed out of bed in the morning until the moment he fell asleep next to his Golden Retriever, Lucy. His coach didn't always understand the words Sebastian used, especially the dog words. Coach often made Sebastian do thirty sit-ups or run ten times around the field if he talked too much.

Lucy was Sebastian's second problem in soccer. She liked to fetch balls while she kept him company on the soccer field--but the balls were supposed to land in the goal, not in her teeth.

She was quick on her paws and could beat any player to the ball. Her sharp fangs often popped the ball into a flat blob of rubber.

That's just what Lucy did one day in the middle of a practice game. Sebastian's team was behind by one. Sebastian was racing down the field, all ready to kick the ball into the goal, when Lucy galloped in and nabbed the ball out from under his feet. She leapt up, pushed the ball above her with her nose, and sank her teeth in.

"Great catch from our best player!" cheered Sebastian.

"Great paw-mouth coordination! She deserves a pup-sicle!"

Coach wrinkled his forehead. Lucy took a big bite out of the ball.

Whoooooosh. Out went the air.

Coach frowned. "Team meeting under the Old Oak," he announced.

Oh-no, thought Sebastian. Coach Danny called team meetings when he needed to talk about really important, really bad things--like bullying, disrespect, bad choices, being a blabbermouth, and hogging the ball.

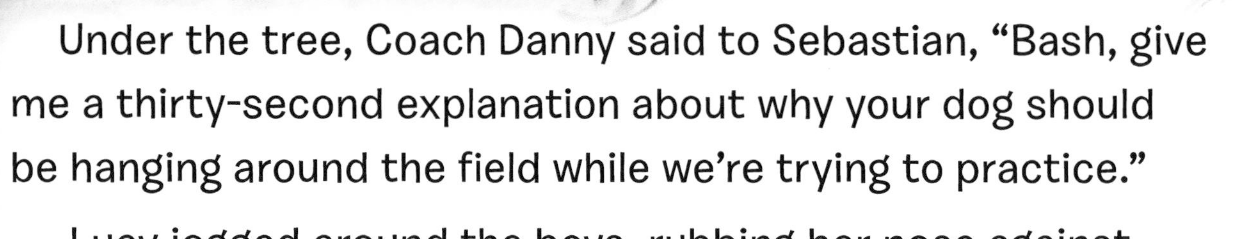

Under the tree, Coach Danny said to Sebastian, “Bash, give me a thirty-second explanation about why your dog should be hanging around the field while we’re trying to practice.”

Lucy jogged around the boys, rubbing her nose against each boy’s hand. They all patted her. Sebastian touched Lucy’s fur, for good luck, while the words raced out of his mouth.

“With Lucy’s paws running beside me, I get a great wagging feeling that makes me play well. My feet go faster,” said Sebastian.

“What?” said Coach.

“Me too!” said Adam, Sebastian’s best friend. “With Lucy close by, I feel like she’s cheering for me. I play better.” Adam always helped Sebastian by explaining his dog words to Coach.

“When the other pack has the ball, I feel Lucy think ‘left’ or ‘right.’ I just watch her canine cues, and know where to run,” said Sebastian.

“Huh?’ said Coach.

“She’s so quick she knows where the ball is going before we do,” explained Adam.

“When I goof up, I pet Lucy and I feel like rolling over with my tongue hanging out instead of crying,” said Sebastian.

“Yes! I pet Lucy after I make mistakes to feel better,” explained Adam.

Coach frowned. Bash thought about soccer without Lucy, and it made his stomach ache. He felt like hanging his head low.

"Coach doesn't have a dog," said Adam.

Lucy sat down and tried to eat the ball, leaving bites of white rubber all over the grass. She licked her lips and let out a loud burp.

Adam's twin, Matthew, giggled. "Lucy makes me laugh, and that makes me happy!"

Coach Danny didn't look impressed. "That's it!" Coach growled. "I don't care how many smooches, sillies, or valentines that dog gives you. Take her home now, Bash! Team, get on the field for a practice game!" He pulled a brand new ball out of his equipment bag.

Now Sebastian's stomach really hurt. Without Lucy, he would feel clumsy and wrong, he thought. He grabbed Lucy by the collar and ran the two blocks home to put her inside. He already missed Lucy's drool on his face, the wet-and-wavy feel of her ears against his cheek, and the sound of her paws trotting beside him.

When he returned to the field, Sebastian said, “Coach, without Lucy here to make everyone wag, you’re going to have to put the team into a down stay.”

Adam started to explain, “You can put a dog into a down stay when he’s acting wild, or jumping up, or doing other bad things....”

Just then Matthew charged into Adam.

Adam yelled at Matthew, “Don’t you knock me over again! That’s not teamwork!”

“You didn’t pass to me, meatball! You need to pass the ball!” Adam said. “Ball-hogging is a Bad Choice.”

“You’re the big ball hog,” Matthew said. “Why should I give you the ball? You’ll never give it back.”

“Hey guys,” Coach Danny said, “what’s gotten into you?”

Matthew pushed Adam and Adam shoved him back. Adam gave the ball an angry kick—a kick so hard that the ball rolled out of bounds, past the oak tree, down the big hill, through the playground, and into the street, where a car rolled over it.

Pop! went the ball. *Whoosh!* it went, as the air swept out of it. The boys stopped fighting and gaped at the flat hunk of rubber in the road.

“Lucy could have nabbed that ball,” Sebastian said. “She’s a fast fetcher, and always ignores distractions–like other dogs yapping on the sidelines. Best of all, she never whines or barks if she makes a mistake and has kisses for everyone.”

“She’s quick, positive, and always nice to everyone–even Coach, who doesn’t have a dog,” explained Adam.

Suddenly a yellow swirl of fur and drool streaked toward them.

"Lucy!" Sebastian said as she kissed his face, nose, and ears. "You smarty-pants, you escaped!" Lucy licked each boy's cheek, one by one. She sat down and peered at Sebastian with dark eyes that were framed on top with randomly spaced eyelashes.

"She sits like that when she's reporting for duty!" Sebastian said. "She's trying to tell us something."

Again, Lucy gave each boy's face a smooch, one by one, ending with Coach Danny, who got a big slobber on his hand.

“She wants us to kiss each other!” Adam yelled. He jumped up and applied his tongue to his brother’s cheek.

“Ugh, get away from me,” Matthew said. “You smell like you’ve been eating Mom’s roasted eggplant.”

“Hold on, guys,” Sebastian said. He leaned toward Lucy and peered into her eyes while she sat patiently in front of him. “She wants us to kiss each other, but not really.”

“She’s trying to share her soccer strategy with us!” said Adam.

Coach Danny shifted his feet and cleared his throat. Lucy sidled up to Coach Danny and gazed up at him with round, feed-me-treats eyes.

"She's asking him to smell her," said Matthew. "That will make him feel good."

"Yes, and she's saying we need kisses and pup-sicles, and to talk to each other with our eyes and our bodies. And we need to feel like a pack," said Sebastian.

"You mean be nice and play like a team," explained Adam.

Sebastian gave Lucy a pat. "And, of course, we need a few treats."

"Yes!" Adam said. "Excellent ideas. Especially the treats!"

"Yeah, Lucy!" The boys cheered, gathering around her.

Coach Danny looked like he was thinking hard.

"What do you think of Lucy's strategy for the pack?" Sebastian asked Coach Danny. He held his breath, waiting for Coach to answer.

Coach Danny smiled. “I get it, guys. With Lucy close by, you feel happier and confident. And confident players go to the top.” He removed his hat, and placed it firmly on Lucy’s head. He dropped his bag of soccer balls at her feet.

“Okay, Lucy-dog, you can coach, too,” he said. “Let’s see where you can take this team with a big slobber and a silly smile.”

Lucy gave Coach's hand a slimy smooch, then peed on his shoe.

The boys laughed. "Let's fetch the ball!" they said, and galloped back to the field, with Lucy nipping at their feet.

ABOUT THE AUTHORS

Lisa Cohn is an award-winning writer and author. Michael Cohn is her son. They live with their family in Portland, Oregon. Visit them at www.BashAndLucy.com and follow "Michael's Dog Blog" for fun dog facts and dog book reviews for kids--from Michael and friends. The blog aims to instill in kids a love of dogs and books.

ABOUT THE ILLUSTRATOR

Heather Nichols is a freelance illustrator who lives where concrete meets moss. Learn more about her at www.YourFaceMyStyle.com.

Made in the USA
Charleston, SC
10 December 2013